My Dad Cancelled Christmas !

Written by Sean Casey
Illustrated by Quinn Casey

COOL KIDS CREATE

NEW YORK

ISBN 978-0-9797297-0-6

FIRST PUBLISHED IN U.S. IN 2007.
THE TEXT WAS SET IN KIDS FONT
PAGE LAYOUT BY ROXANNA ALLEN

COOL KIDS CREATE

NEW YORK

'Twas just hours before Christmas,
Dad was having a bad day;

The car had a flat, the ATM
no cash, he banged his knee,
Things were not going his way.

1

None of us moved an inch when he walked in the front door. We were too busy playing video games to notice the junk strewn across the floor.

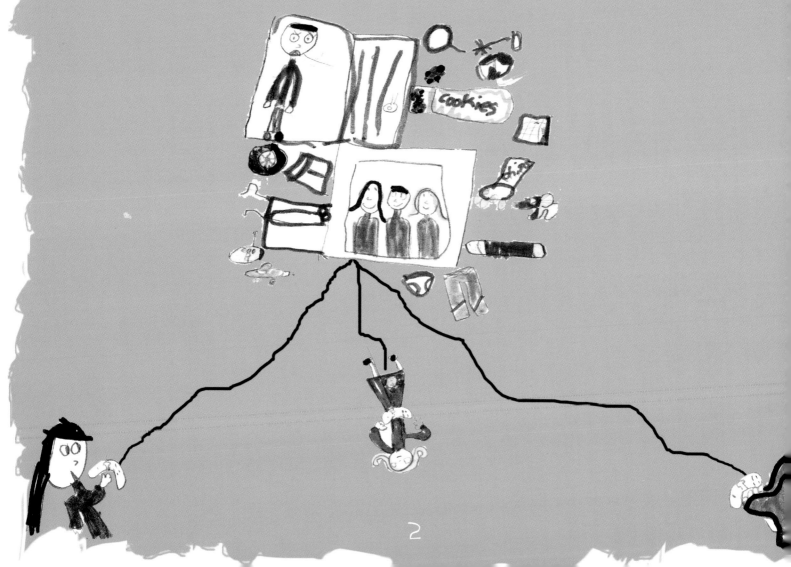

Then Dad tripped over the laundry, piled in a heap;
"Where's your mother!" he yelled, but she was in bed,
fast asleep.

"I have had it this time, you are all spoiled rotten;
You will learn a lesson this year that won't soon be
forgotten."

"I am getting rid of the stockings, the ornaments, the tree; Christmas is cancelled!" he shouted with glee.

He stuffed all of the decorations into a brown box;
"Stockings," he sneered, "were meant to be socks!"

"But you can't stop Santa." My little sister cried.
"How do you know?" he answered, "this is the first
time I've tried."

"When I was your age, we were half poor,
we were happy with whatever Santa left us for
sure."

"We were grateful, I tell you, if we each got one toy,
not hundreds, like you kids, in a week to destroy."

"But we always had food on our table, a roof overhead,
clothes on our backs and a warm bed."

"There are plenty of kids who will get nothing
but hunger and sorrow,
Maybe Santa will bring them your presents
tomorrow."

"Everyone upstairs! Perhaps Santa
will leave us a broom,
to clean up this mess and the
one in your room."

We did not put out cookies or milk as he sent us to bed.
How could there be no Christmas, no Santa, no sled?

We could not believe
he could be such a
grouch;
Finally the house
grew quiet as he fell
asleep on the couch.

11

None of us could sleep, try as we might;
It was then that Mom came into our room
to wish us good night.
"But Mommy," I whimpered, "that's why
we're so sad,
this time he means it that's why he's
so mad."

""So what is it this time that's
got him so crazy?"
"He says we get too many presents,
we're ungrateful and lazy."

12

"I can't even imagine, but for some girls and boys,
he said there would be no presents, no treats
or no toys."
I must admit some of what he said is in fact true
we are all very lucky and so is he too."

"Before you go to sleep remember those souls in your prayers, I'll make sure Dad knows what you are doing when I go downstairs."

Next morning, as usual, I was the first to awake.
I nudged my little brother and gave my sister a shake.
We all were nervous and knew not what to say.
What if Mom failed and Dad had chased Santa away?

When we crept down the steps what was the first thing
for us to see, but Dad still asleep, across from the tree.
Which now stood up straight, and with presents galore,
"Santa came!" we yelled as Dad let out a snore.

"Look Daddy, Daddy!" we hollered with delight,
As his eyes opened wide to take in the sight.
"Christmas is here," Mom's saved the day.
"Santa has come — Hooray! Hooray!"

"When Santa came last night, I told him my position.
Before you open your presents, please sit down and listen."
"He heard of the prayers that you said before bed,
how you did not pray for toys for yourselves but
for others instead."

"Over cookies and milk, he said I should not be so stressed,
you guys are only young once and I'm truly blessed."
"With a twitch of his nose and a tip to his brow,
he fixed this place up to be as you see it now."

"But before he left he turned one last time to your Dad,
and said, 'as to you an important lesson is to be had.'"

"When it comes to Christmas" he warned, "you leave that to me." Just then Mom came down the stairs and said, "I agree."

"I agree!"

Dad let out a smile and gave his shoulders a shrug,
He pulled us all together in a big hug.

"Cancelling Christmas, I must have sound like a scrooge,
a mean old grinch or most likely a stooge."
"Now let's open the presents without further ado,
I love you all and a Merry Christmas, too."

24

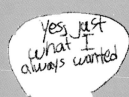

About the author: Sean Casey. The father of Quinn, Caleigh and Jack, Sean is an attorney admitted to the state bars of New York and Connecticut. My Dad Cancelled Christmas was completed with illustrations in 2005. The Casey's currently reside in Breezy Point, New York.

About the illustrator: Quinn Casey. Quinn is currently a fifth grader at St. Francis DeSales grammar school in Belle Harbor, Queens County, New York City. Quinn sings in her parish choir and plays on basketball, softball, soccer, volleyball and swimming teams.